HORSELAND

HarperCollins®, ☙®, and HarperEntertainment™ are trademarks of HarperCollins Publishers.

Horseland #6: If the Horseshoe Fits
Copyright © 2008 DIC Entertainment Corp.
Horseland property ™ Horseland LLC
Printed in the United States of Americaa.

www.harpercollinschildrens.com
www.horseland.com

Library of Congress catalog card number: 2007942471
ISBN 978-0-06-134172-4

Book design by Sean Boggs
❖
First Edition

HORSELAND

6

If the Horseshoe Fits

Adapted by
ANNIE AUERBACH
Based on the episode
"FIRST LOVE"
Written by
JIM PERONTO

📖HarperEntertainment
An Imprint of HarperCollinsPublishers

CHAPTER 1

It's a beautiful spring day at Horseland. In the trees that surround the expansive ranch, birds chirp happily as they fly from branch to branch. Located in a picturesque area with mountains on one side and a forest on the other, Horseland is a wonderful place to train and board a horse. Perhaps the best thing of all is this well-kept secret: All the animals can talk to one another—and the humans have no idea!

This particular day, Angora the feisty cat sits in the grass under the shade of a large tree, licking her fur. An energetic, potbellied pig named Teeny interrupts her thoughts.

"Hi, Angora," Teeny says, as she stands directly in front of the cat. "Why do you spend so much time preening and grooming? And then preening and grooming some more?" The pig with the pink ribbon on her tail is usually curious, and this time is no exception.

Angora rolls her eyes and sighs. "Don't you know anything, Teeny?" she asks and licks her paw again. "Nothing matters more than looking good."

"Oh, I didn't know!" Teeny replies. She looks concerned. "Why doesn't anybody tell me these things?" Teeny drops her head down, disappointed and upset. Suddenly, she brightens. "I have an idea! Can you teach me how to do it, Angora?" Teeny runs around excitedly. She nuzzles up to Angora. "Please, oh please, oh please?"

Angora gives a weary sigh. She can't see a way out of this. "All right, keep your tail on!" Angora says, pushing the pig away.

"Yippee! Oh, goody goody!" Teeny cheers and runs in a circle happily.

"First, you lick your paw—or hoof—or whatever," began Angora. She demonstrates on her own paw.

"Okay, okay! First, I lick," her eager student says, and proceeds to lick her hoof with quick little licks.

"No, no, no, Teeny," Angora tells her, shaking her head. "Long and slow."

"Oh, I get it," says Teeny. She looks seriously at Angora, a newfound pride in her eyes. "This takes some concentration." Then the pig takes a *very* long lick.

At that moment, Shep the dog walks by and notices the pair licking in unison. "Now I've seen everything," the Australian shepherd says, quite confused. He goes over to them.

"Teeny, what are you doing?" Shep asks.

He can't imagine why the pig is licking her hooves.

"I'm preening, Shep," Teeny says proudly in between licks. "Angora told me looking pretty is what matters most."

Shep shakes his head. "Actually, Teeny, it's not."

Angora looks up. "Excuuuuse me?"

"It's who you are *inside* that counts," explains Shep. He looks out into the distance. "Alma found that out not so long ago. . . ."

"I smell a story coming on," Angora says, rolling her eyes. She knows Shep well.

Teeny sniffs the air. "I don't smell anything," the pig says innocently.

Shep smiles broadly and begins to tell the tale. . . .

CHAPTER 2

One warm, cloudless day, a pair of butterflies circled each other, dancing on the wind. On a tree trunk, two squirrels playfully chased each other. Below, in the lush rolling hills, two skunks gazed fondly into each other's eyes, while a gentle doe and a strong buck nuzzled nearby. There was definitely something in the air: It was love.

Suddenly, the doe and the buck heard a pounding noise. It grew stronger and louder by the second. The pair took off across the meadow just as a horse and rider came thundering through the bushes.

It was Alma Rodriguez, sitting atop Button, her skewbald pinto mare. The twelve-year-old girl was covered in dirt and mud as she joyfully rode Button at top speed across the hillside.

"Woo-hoo!" Alma cried, as they came to

a stop. "Hey, you really showed 'em what you're made of, didn't you, *chica*?" She affectionately patted her horse on the neck.

Button whinnied proudly in agreement.

At that moment, the other girls rode up. Molly Washington reined in Calypso, her spotted Appaloosa mare, as Sarah Whitney and her horse stopped alongside Alma.

"You *are* good, Alma," said Sarah. Even atop Scarlet, her black Arabian mare, Sarah couldn't catch Alma on this type of terrain.

"Thanks," replied Alma as she dismounted. An eager look spread across her face. "Let's have a rope-twirling contest!" She pulled out a rope from her saddlebag and began to twirl it skillfully.

The other two girls, Chloe and Zoey Stilton, sighed dramatically. The sisters were rich and snobby—and proud of it. Doing something as common as rope twirling made the girls roll their eyes. It wasn't only the girls who were stuck up—so were their horses. Pepper, Zoey's horse, was a gray

Dutch Warmblood mare with an attitude, and Chili, Chloe's horse, was a gray Dutch Warmblood stallion with a serious mean streak.

Just then, they heard more galloping sounds. The girls turned to see Will Taggert riding toward them on Jimber, his golden palomino stallion. Will wasn't supposed to be along for the ride, and everyone wondered why he was there.

Will reined in Jimber and came to a stop next to Alma.

"Hey, Alma! Been looking all over for you," Will said.

"Are you sure you weren't looking for *me*, Will?" Zoey asked flirtatiously.

"Or me?" asked Chloe, twirling a lock of strawberry blond hair around her finger. The two batted their eyes at Will.

But Will didn't pay them any attention. "Yeah, I'm sure," he said with a shrug. Then he dismounted and walked up to Alma. He held out a letter that was smudged with dirt.

"What is it, Will?" asked Alma.

"I just found this by the mailbox," Will explained. "Looks like it's been sitting in the dirt a few days. Somebody must have dropped it."

Alma took the letter and looked at it closely. "It's postmarked two weeks ago," she realized. Then she gasped. "And it's from *Alejandro*!"

The other girls exchanged a confused look.

"Who's *Alejandro*?" asked Zoey.

"Alexander—my pen pal," explained Alma.

"I didn't know you had a pen pal, Alma," said Sarah, pushing her blond hair out of her eyes.

"Neither did I," Molly said. Then she rode Calypso over to Alma and eagerly asked, "What's he like?"

A dreamy look crossed Alma's face. "Pretty awesome, that's all," she gushed, clutching the letter to her chest.

Alma went on to explain that her pen pal had a horse named Bucephalus. "It's the same name as Alexander the Great's horse," she told everyone. "I read that in *The Secret Life of Horses*."

Chloe looked doubtful. "What's so great about *this* Alexander?" she asked.

"His dad's in the entertainment industry," replied Alma. "They travel all the time."

Zoey and Chloe's eyes lit up with sudden interest. If Alexander traveled all the time, then he must be rich. That was just their type of boy!

"Tell us more!" Zoey insisted, leaning forward in her saddle.

Alma was happy to oblige. "He's a great horseman . . . been to the state championship three times," she said.

Molly and Sarah looked at each other, impressed. This was far more interesting than whether or not Alexander had money.

Alma opened the letter and quickly read it. Suddenly, her smile fell away. "Wait a minute," she said, a hint of worry in her voice. "This can't be right." She looked at her friends, panic growing inside of her. "This says he's coming to visit Horseland— TODAY!"

CHAPTER 3

Later that morning, the stable was buzzing with activity. Zoey, Chloe, Molly, and Sarah were all busy grooming their horses, and the horses loved the attention.

"Psst!"

Molly looked around, but she didn't see anyone.

"Psst!"

Molly looked around again as Calypso snorted. Still nobody.

"Molly! Over here!" said the voice.

Molly turned to see Alma peeking around the stable door, motioning to her. She wondered why Alma was being so secretive—and weird.

"Is Alexander here yet?" Alma whispered.

Molly shook her head. "No, not yet," she answered.

Alma breathed a quick sigh of relief. "Good," she said, and walked into the stable. She led in Button behind her. "Does anyone know someone with a fast car? I need to go far, far away."

Molly was confused. "What's the matter, Alma?" she asked her friend. "Don't you want to finally meet him?"

"He's rich, well traveled, an expert horseman . . . he's practically a prince!" declared Alma. She frowned and looked down at the ground. Her voice became quiet. "What's he going to think when he sees I'm so plain . . . so average?"

Just then, Chloe and Zoey walked up to her.

"You have a point, Alma," said Chloe, her hands on her hips.

"Yeah," agreed her freckle-faced sister. "We'll take care of your rich, princely friend," said Zoey, with a determined look in her eyes.

Molly saw Alma's face fall and quickly

placed her hands reassuringly on Alma's shoulders. "Oh, don't listen to them," she said. She gave her a supportive squeeze. "There's a princess inside you. All we need to do is let her out. Come on! You'll see!"

Alma felt hopeful. *Is Molly right?* she wondered. *Is there someone inside me who would be good enough for Alexander?*

CHAPTER 4

Molly led Alma indoors to the dressing room on the second floor of the ranch house. This was the place where everyone got ready for horse competitions and shows. There were multiple stations, each with a chair, a large mirror, and various hair care products and lotions. In one corner stood an armoire and a folding screen to change behind. Magnificent green chandeliers hung overhead. Perhaps best of all—for today, at

least—was the fact that it was private and no one would hear Molly and Alma as they prepared for Alexander's visit.

"First, we work on introductions," Molly began, closing the door behind her. "As you know from competition, there's no such thing as a second impression."

"Right," said Alma. She wrung her hands anxiously. Molly kept encouraging her to relax, but it wasn't working.

"Now, pretend I'm Alexander," Molly said.

Alma giggled. With her black hair pulled up in a ponytail on the top of her head, Molly definitely didn't look like a boy. But Alma played along anyway.

Molly cleared her throat and extended her hand. She lowered her voice to sound like a boy and said, "Hello, there. I'm Alexander."

"Uh . . . ," said Alma, feeling flustered. She shook Molly's hand. "I'm, um, mama mala-ma. . . ." She laughed nervously.

"Oh, well. There's room for improvement, " Molly said supportively.

Alma looked at her feet. She felt embarrassed and silly. "It's hopeless," she said, sadly shaking her head.

"Look, Alma, you're an incredible person," Molly told her. "You've just got to show it!"

Alma was grateful for Molly's support, but she didn't have any clue how she was supposed to "show it."

Luckily, Molly had some ideas! First, she showed Alma how to walk across a room with confidence. Alma caught on quickly and walked across the room like a fashion model on the runway.

"Remember, it's all attitude," Molly reminded her.

Alma tossed her hair and looked over her shoulder. "Whatever!" she said confidently.

"All right!" Molly cheered. "The girl's got it going on!" She gave Alma a thumbs-up and big smile.

21

A hopeful Alma smiled at Molly. "Are you sure?" she asked.

"Sure I'm sure!" Molly replied. "You'll be ready when Alexander the Great rolls up."

Just then, the girls heard something outside. They rushed to the window and saw a station wagon pull up with a horse trailer attached to the rear.

Alexander had arrived!

Alma was so nervous that she gasped and dropped to the floor. Then, very slowly, she rose up and peeked out the window. She bit her nails nervously.

Outside, the car door opened.

"He's getting out!" Molly said excitedly. She couldn't wait to see what Alexander looked like. *For Alma to be so nervous, he must look like a movie star!* Molly thought.

But Alexander wasn't what she expected—at all. A thin, geeky boy with dark hair got out

23

of the car. He took out a handkerchief and cleaned his thick, square glasses. He sneezed and blew his nose with a loud honk.

"*That's* him?!" asked Molly. She couldn't believe that Alma was gaga over this nerdy boy with freckles.

"That's him," Alma declared dreamily. "Isn't he hubba hibba bibbaba . . ." She was

so lovesick, she could hardly speak!

Molly tried to shake Alma out of her blubbering state. "Come on, Alma! Snap out of it! You've got to deal with it."

Alma stood up and began pacing in circles. "What am I going to do?" she said frantically. She began to pace faster until, finally, her panic overtook her and she felt she had to get out of there. "Molly, I can't do this. I . . . I . . . I have to return a library book that's way overdue," Alma said, and quickly ran out of the room.

Molly scratched her head. She knew Alma was nervous about meeting her pen pal, but she couldn't understand why her friend would react like this.

Down below, Sarah, Zoey, and Chloe ran down the path toward the car. Sarah couldn't wait to meet Alexander. Zoey and Chloe couldn't wait to meet Alexander's money!

"Hello, there!" Sarah called as they approached. Although Sarah's family had a lot of money, she valued friendship first and foremost . . . unlike Chloe and Zoey.

"Um, hi," replied Alexander.

This can't be Alexander, Chloe thought. *He's too nerdy.* She looked inside the car to see if anyone else was in it.

Alexander was perplexed. "Can I help you find something?" he asked Chloe.

"More like some*one*," replied Chloe. "Who are you?"

"Chloe! Don't be rude!" said Zoey, pushing her sister out of the way. Zoey walked up to the boy and made a somewhat more polite attempt to find out who he was. "Hi! Welcome to Horseland. I'm Zoey . . . and you are?"

The boy cleared his throat and said, "I'm

Alexander Buglik."

"You're Alexander?!" Zoey and Chloe asked in shock.

"Yeah," the boy answered. "I'm . . . I'm here to meet Alma. "Did she mention me?" He looked expectantly from one girl to the other.

Zoey and Chloe turned to each other and giggled.

"Well, sort of," said Zoey. She and her sister couldn't believe that *this* was the boy that Alma had been talking about.

"Is it okay if I let my horse out now?" asked Alexander. "He needs to stretch after that drive."

"Sure," replied Sarah.

Nearby in the stable, the horses were watching and listening.

"I don't see why Alma's so nervous about meeting her pen pal," Button said to Calypso.

They looked on as Alexander opened the horse trailer and led his horse down the ramp. Bucephalus was a large, impressive black stallion with a white blaze on his forehead. The handsome horse shook his mane and neighed.

Suddenly, Button gasped. "Hepapa depapa dopa peepa," she babbled. Just like her rider, Button was smitten with the new arrival!

CHAPTER 6

Alexander waved good-bye to his parents as they drove off. They would return at the end of the day to pick him up. Meanwhile, Bucephalus was enjoying being the center of attention with the other kids at Horseland.

"You're a good-looking guy, Bucephalus," Sarah told the horse, as she patted his nose.

Bucephalus whinnied happily at the compliment.

Just then, Will and his cousin Bailey Handler walked up and joined the group.

"Whoa! Check out that horse!" exclaimed Bailey, looking at the commanding creature in front of him. Bailey's parents owned Horseland, so he had seen his fair share of horses over the years.

"Pretty impressive, kid," Will said to Alexander.

"Why, thank you," said Alexander. "His name's Bucephalus. He's from a long line of stallions bred for strength and endurance."

"Wow!" Will said, and smiled.

"Yeah," agreed Bailey. "That's definitely *wow*-worthy."

Alexander began to fidget. "Um, is Alma here?" he asked shyly. "I'd really like to, you know, meet her."

Close by, Molly whispered to Sarah.

"Alma's gone AWOL," Molly said, trying to keep her voice quiet. "We're going to have to stall."

But Alexander overheard. "Stall?" he asked.

Sarah thought quickly. "Stall! We have to prepare a stall for Bucephalus . . . for him to stay in while he's here!" She laughed nervously, hoping that her cover-up was believable. She pulled Will aside and whispered, "You and Bailey show Alexander around while we try to find Alma."

Will nodded and turned to the boy. "Hey, Alexander, how'd you like to go for a ride around the grounds?"

"Yeah," Bailey chimed in. "We can go up in the hills, too." Bailey loved to ride hard through the rough terrain on Aztec, his Kiger mustang stallion.

"Well, I think Bucephalus is kind of worn-out from that drive," said Alexander nervously. "Maybe later, okay?" He took out his handkerchief and blew his nose again.

"Sure, we got plenty of time," said Will. "Come on. We'll show you around." He and Bailey led Alexander toward the arena.

A little while later, Alexander watched as Will and Bailey rode their horses around a course inside the arena. Will and Jimber successfully jumped over a gate and then a wall. Bailey and Aztec sailed over a combination of a hedge and a railing called an oxer.

Alexander was astonished. "Amazing!" he exclaimed. The boys made it look so easy. Alexander sighed heavily. "I wish I could ride like that," he said quietly. He looked around to make sure no one had heard him. He didn't want anyone to find out his secret.

CHAPTER 7

"**A**lma?" called Sarah.

"Alma, are you in here?" Zoey asked.

The girls, along with Molly and Chloe, were in the stable looking for Alma. They had searched the cafeteria, the arena, and the ranch house. But Alma wasn't in any of those places. The stable wasn't looking promising until some hay fell on Molly's head from the loft above. Molly smiled. She cleared her throat to get the other girls'

attention as she pointed up with her finger. The others instantly understood, and they all climbed the ladder into the loft.

Once up there, they looked at the hay piles and noticed that one particular pile looked strange. They pulled the hay apart and found Alma sitting there, reading *The Secret Life of Horses*. Alma gasped with surprise.

"Alma! What are you doing here?" asked Molly.

"Oh, reading," Alma replied, trying to sound as if reading in a pile of hay were the most natural thing in the world. But the looks from the other girls flustered her, and she began to babble. "*The Secret Life of Horses* . . . love this book . . . real page-turner. Did you know that Alexander the Great's horse was a black stallion born in 331 BC?"

Chloe was confused. "Wait. Don't you want to meet Alexander the *guest*?"

"Oh, yeah," said Alma. She gave a half-smile. "I forgot he was here. This book is *that* good."

But Molly and Sarah weren't convinced.

Alma sighed and revealed the truth: "I'm not ready. Sorry."

Just then, Zoey piped up. "I think Chloe and I can help," she said confidently.

"Right!" agreed Chloe. Her eyes lit up at the prospect. "We know exactly what you need."

Alma looked at the sisters with hesitation. Could they really help her?

CHAPTER 8

Chloe and Zoey led Alma inside the ranch house to the dressing room. Once there, Alma looked woefully in the mirror. She didn't like her reflection one bit. All she saw was someone who was plain and boring. Alma couldn't imagine that Alexander would be impressed, and she didn't think she could face him. She figured if she kept hiding out, he'd eventually leave and she'd be off the hook.

But Chloe and Zoey had other plans.

They stood behind Alma and looked excitedly at their new "project." They couldn't
wait to start transforming Alma's look.

"Okay, just leave everything to the style
sisters," Zoey told her, grinning.

"That's right! It's our turn now," said
Chloe, as she led Alma toward the sink.

Once Alma was seated in a chair, Chloe

covered her with a smock to protect her clothes from getting wet. Alma leaned back in the chair while Chloe turned on the water to wet Alma's hair. Chloe squirted some shampoo into one hand and then applied it to Alma's hair, lathering it up. After all the shampoo was rinsed out, it was time to blow-dry. Because Alma had long, thick hair, it took two superpowered hair dryers to get the job done.

But that was just the beginning. Zoey took Alma's hair and twisted it in all different directions, securing it with clips. Then Chloe applied long, fake eyelashes. They slathered vibrant pink lipstick onto Alma's lips and dabbed blue shadow onto her eyelids. Then the sisters decked Alma out in jewelry. Around her neck was a golden, gaudy necklace. Huge, flashy earrings completed the look. The only problem was, Alma wasn't sure this was the look she wanted.

Chloe and Zoey stepped back and took a look at their creation. They studied Alma intently. "Hmm . . ."

"Nope," said Chloe, shaking her head.

"Nuh-uh," said Zoey. Something wasn't right.

It was Alma's clothes. They thought she needed to trade her riding boots and vest for something trendy and hip. Zoey knew just the thing. She ran out of the room. When she returned, she handed Alma a box and motioned for her to change behind the

dressing screen. Alma looked hesitant but agreed. A few minutes later, Alma emerged in a very *unique* outfit. . . .

She wore a green fitted shirt and a lilac ruffled skirt with a belt cinched at the waist. On her legs were white tights and tall, purple boots with black straps and buckles all the way up to her knees.

Chloe and Zoey stood together, hands rubbing their chins, studying Alma's new look. "Hmm," they said in unison.

"No," said Chloe, shaking her head.

"Wrong," said Zoey, agreeing with her sister.

They ran up to Alma and changed some things around. They swapped out the green shirt and put her in cropped green pants. Then Alma's hair was let loose to hang around her shoulders. Once again, the sisters stepped back for another look. "Hmm . . ."

"Perfect!" declared Zoey. The transformation was complete!

"*Now* you're ready to meet Alexander,"

said Chloe. She pulled a mirror over so Alma could see the makeover.

Dizzy from the whole process, Alma wearily looked in the mirror. "Aaaah!" she screamed. She didn't recognize the girl staring back at her. It was as if she were looking at the bride of Frankenstein. One thing was certain: She knew she had to get out of there before Chloe and Zoey did anything else to her! Alma ran out of the room in complete terror and desperation.

"*Now* what's wrong with her?" Zoey asked her sister.

Chloe shrugged. "Guess she's not used to high fashion."

CHAPTER 9

Just after Alma fled the dressing room, Bailey and Alexander entered through a different door. Bailey looked around the room, his eyes finally resting on Chloe and Zoey.

"Hey, have you two seen Alma?" Bailey asked the sisters.

Alexander looked around and smiled bashfully. "I'm really looking forward to meeting her," he revealed.

"You just missed her," Chloe told them

and looked at her sister, her eyes wide.

Zoey had to think fast. "She went to . . . uh . . . return a library book."

"You can stay with us in the meantime," suggested Chloe. She gave Alexander a coy smile.

"Yeah," said Zoey. "You must have lots of interesting stories about the places you've been."

Alexander gulped as Zoey and Chloe closed in on him.

"The people you've met," said Chloe.

"The money your dad has," said Zoey. As always, she was drawn to anyone who was rich.

Alexander became nervous and flustered. "Yeah . . . uh . . . er . . . I have been to a lot of places," he stuttered.

Luckily, Bailey came to the rescue. "You don't want to be here yakkin' with them, Al. Let's go for that ride now. What do you say?"

Alexander looked uneasy. "Um, yeah, sure thing," he said hesitantly. He knew he

had to get out of there. "Just let me . . . uh . . . go check something first." He made a beeline for the door and ran out.

Bailey shook his head, perplexed. "I don't understand that guy," he said.

Behind him, Chloe and Zoey were disappointed. First, their plan to transform Alma wasn't appreciated, and now the rich boy didn't want to have anything to do with them.

What is wrong with everybody today? Chloe thought, as she and Zoey headed outside.

Meanwhile in the stables, the horses were getting to know Alexander's horse, Bucephalus.

Button leaned out from her stall. "How do you like Horseland?" she asked the stallion.

"It's very nice," replied Bucephalus. "It's not what I'm used to."

Across the way, Chili gave a snort. "I guess you're used to fancier stuff." He assumed the black stallion was used to living in luxury. Chili himself would have liked to be living in luxury.

Bucephalus was surprised by Chili's comment. "Oh, no," he answered. "This is the nicest place I've ever seen."

The other horses traded puzzled looks. What was he talking about?

"It is?" asked Button. She didn't understand at all.

Chili was confused, too. "But you're a

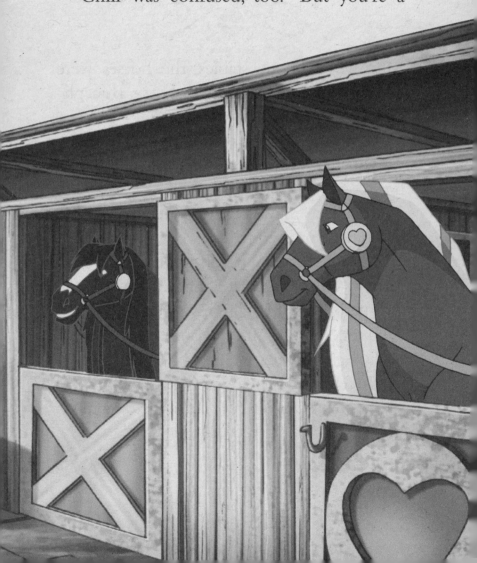

champ," he said to Bucephalus. "You were at state three times, right?"

Bucephalus cocked his head in confusion. "I'm not quite sure what you mean."

"You know, state championship? We heard you went three times," said Chili.

Bucephalus shook his head. "I never went to a state championship," he explained. "I work in a traveling carnival—pulling a carriage ride."

Chili and the horses were shocked at this revelation.

"Wait a minute," Chili said. "What about all the things we've heard?"

"What do you mean?" asked Bucephalus.

"You know," replied Button, "about Alexander being really rich and—"

Bucephalus shook his head. "His family's not rich. They work in the carnival. They're *wonderful* people, but they aren't rich."

The truth was out—and the horses were stunned.

"We thought that kid was an expert

horseman!" Button confessed.

A loud chuckle came from Bucephalus's mouth. What the other horses thought couldn't have been further from the truth. "Alexander gets most of his knowledge of horses from books," he explained.

All the horses couldn't believe their ears. *I knew something was fishy!* Chili thought.

"My, my, my!" Button said in disbelief.

The horses now knew the truth . . . but what about their riders?

CHAPTER 10

When Alexander hurriedly left the dressing room, he wasn't sure where to go. He just knew he had to stay out of sight for a while. He ducked into the stable, checking over his shoulder to make sure no one had followed him.

Inside the stable, all the horses neighed.

Alexander was puzzled. "Boy, these horses sure are noisy for some reason," he said to himself. Little did Alexander know that *he*

was the reason for the commotion!

Then Alexander saw a perfect hiding spot—up the ladder, in the hayloft. Once he climbed up, he found quite a surprise: A girl was sitting there reading a book. It was Alma! She was still dressed in her garish outfit, her hair and makeup completely overdone.

"Oh! Hello!" said Alexander, laughing nervously. "You spooked me."

Alma looked around for a way out, but there was no escape. She'd have to speak to him. "Er—um—uh—hi—what—what are you doing up here?" she asked, standing up.

"Well, I was just looking for somewhere to read," Alexander replied.

Alma brightened. "You like to read?" she asked with a smile.

Alexander smiled back. "Oh, yeah, love it," he admitted. "When I'm not reading . . . I'm usually reading!" He laughed, and Alma did as well.

"Me too!" said Alma. "I mean, I also love

riding horses, but reading's so much fun."

"Yeah, horses are pretty amazing, aren't they?" said Alexander. "My pen pal, Alma, loves horses, too. Do you know her?"

Alma realized that Alexander didn't know who she was! "Um, you could say we're very close," Alma replied, smiling to herself.

"She seems so real, so genuine," Alexander said, thinking of the letters she had written to him. "That's what I want—a true friend, you know?"

Alma bowed her head, feeling a bit ashamed. "Yeah," she said quietly.

Alexander continued, "Not like those sisters—Zoey and Chloe. Hate to say it, but they're such phonies."

Alma squirmed uncomfortably. "Phonies. Right," she said with a sigh. Then she started toward the ladder.

"Where are you going?" asked Alexander. He tried to stop her, but Alma continued climbing down the ladder.

"Nice talking to you!" she called.

Alexander looked over the edge of the loft. "Wait! Do you have to go?" he asked.

"Yeah, sorry. Bye!" replied Alma, as she ran through the stable. Once again, Alma had cold feet.

"Please, come back!" shouted Alexander. "I don't even know your name!"

But Alma wasn't stopping for anything or anybody. She grabbed her riding helmet and ran over to Button's stall. She quickly led her horse out of the stall, hopped on, and took off. Alexander hurried down the ladder, but he was too late.

Alma and Button exited the stable just as Sarah, Molly, Chloe, and Zoey walked in.

"Aaahhh!" screamed the girls. They jumped back in surprise as the horse thundered past them.

Molly and Sarah stared after Alma. They couldn't believe their eyes.

"Whoa! What happened to her?" Molly asked.

"What do you mean?" asked Zoey.

"She never looked better," said Chloe.

"Wait! Please!" shouted Alexander, running out of the stable.

But it didn't work. Alma just kept riding, sending up spirals of dirt and dust behind her.

"Alma!" Sarah called out. "Where are you going?"

"What?" asked Alexander, doing a double take. "*That* was Alma?"

Molly nodded. "That was her, all right What is going on around here?"

There was no time to explain. Alexander ran back inside the stable and put on a riding helmet. He took Bucephalus's reins and led him out of the stall.

"Easy, boy," Alexander said tentatively.
Bucephalus was curious about where they
were going.

"Giddyup!" Alexander said, once he was in the saddle. Then he rode out of the stable, bouncing around and holding on for dear life. "Wait, Alma! Wait!" he called. He had to find her!

CHAPTER 11

Alma rode furiously through the gates of Horseland and into the forest beyond. She headed up to a mountain ridge that was dotted with a few trees and shrubs. Button expertly galloped across the rocky terrain, trying not to think about the ravine below. The running water from the powerful stream beneath them was flowing fast and furious that day. Tears rolled down Alma's face. She felt absolutely horrible.

"Oh, I really blew it, Button," she cried. "I'm one of those phonies he can't stand!"

As Button continued up the ridge, the ground cracked a bit in certain places. But neither Button nor Alma noticed. Alma was lost in her own little world.

"Why was I such a fool?" she moaned. "I'll never be able to show my face around him." As she took Button farther up the ridge, she suddenly heard something . . .

or was it someone?

"Alma! Come back!"

It was Alexander! He had almost caught up to her! Because he wasn't an experienced rider, he bounced around in the saddle and was having a hard time navigating Bucephalus through the rugged terrain.

Alma pulled on Button's reins to stop her horse. She turned to see Alexander round the corner. Suddenly, disaster struck! He and Bucephalus crossed the same piece of shaky terrain that Alma had crossed—and it cracked even more. The rock broke apart, sending Alexander and his horse sliding down the ravine!

"Almaaaaa!" cried Alexander as Bucephalus neighed in panic. They were both very frightened.

Button whinnied worriedly, and Alma called to Alexander. But Bucephalus continued to struggle to gain his footing on the rocky slope. The situation was getting worse by the second.

"Help, Alma!" shouted Alexander.

From above, Alma and Button looked on in distress. "We've got to help them, Button!" Alma declared.

Just then, Sarah, Will, Bailey, Molly, Zoey, and Chloe rode up to the edge of a cliff located on the opposite side of the ravine.

"Oh, no!" exclaimed Sarah. "Look down there!"

All the riders looked where Sarah was pointing. They saw Alexander and Bucephalus attempting to climb back up the incline. But it wasn't working; they just kept sliding back down.

At that moment, Alma rode over to the edge of the ridge. She tried to get a closer look, but her sticky fake eyelashes got stuck together.

"Argh! I can't see!" she said in exasperation. "Why did I ever let them put these on me in the first place?" Then, without wasting another moment, she pulled off the fake eyelashes, took off the earrings and necklace, and wiped off the lipstick. She took a deep breath, and a look of determination crossed her face as she finally felt like herself again.

Across the way, Molly suspected what Alma was going to do next. "Don't do it, Alma," she said, even though she knew Alma couldn't hear her. "It's too dangerous." She

65

was worried for her friend. Sarah tried to reassure her and reminded her that if anyone could make this rescue, it was Alma.

Slowly and skillfully, Alma led Button sideways down the slope, cautiously finding stable rocks to step on. Alexander and Bucephalus were still trying to scramble back up, but the ravine was too steep. Bucephalus was getting tired, and Alexander was becoming even more worried. Just below them, water rushed past, providing no exit.

"Come on, Button," Alma said to her horse. Her voice was calm and steady. "If we're going to save them, we're going to have to do better than this."

Button neighed in agreement and set off. Nimbly, the horse negotiated the slope toward the endangered pair. They worked together well. Alma trusted Button. If only Alma had trusted herself as much.

"Alma! Help!" Alexander called again, as he and Bucephalus slipped farther down.

Alma stayed focused and encouraged Button. "Come on, girl. We've got to make it to that ledge."

Back across the ravine, the others held their breath as they watched the action unfold. Everyone was nervous for Alma and Button.

"She's going to go for it!" Bailey realized.

Molly covered her face with her hands. "I can't watch!"

"We have to help her!" insisted Bailey. He couldn't just stand around.

Sarah shook her head. "We'd never get there in time," she pointed out.

Bailey grimaced. He knew Sarah was right; he just wished there were something they could do.

They looked out to see Alma and Button making progress. Once Alma reached the flat surface of a small ledge, she'd be safer *and* closer to Alexander and Bucephalus.

"Okay, Button, almost there!" she said, urging the mare closer.

Button slid the last few feet but was quickly able to stabilize herself on the ledge.

"Come on," Alma said to her horse. "This is our last chance!"

There was no time to waste. Alma pressed her heels gently into Button's side, and the horse used what little ground she had to run and leap to another ledge lower down. It was a risky and dangerous move—but it worked.

Alma exhaled a feeling of relief and then quickly dismounted from Button. She pulled a rope from her saddlebag and ran to the edge of the ledge. Expertly, she twirled it above her head.

"Alexander! Catch the rope!" she instructed, as she threw it out toward him.

Alexander caught it on the first try. "Got it!" he cried happily. He looped the end around the pommel on his saddle.

"Good going!" Alma called to him. She threaded the rope through a nearby tree and tied her end to the pommel on her saddle. Then she mounted her horse and said, "Help me out here, Button."

Button whinnied and began to walk forward. The rope tightened between the two saddles as Button grunted and pulled with all of her might. It was a struggle, but Button kept moving forward. Alma looked behind her expectantly. Slowly, Alexander and Bucephalus were pulled up the cliff side. When they reached safety, a round of applause and cheering could be heard from across the ravine.

"She did it!" shouted Sarah. A huge smile and a wave of relief washed over her face.

"Way to go! All right!" exclaimed the others.

Alma had saved the day!

CHAPTER 12

Finally back on level ground, Alexander dismounted Bucephalus and dropped to his knees. He was grateful to be safe, although he felt a bit woozy.

Alma ran over to him and kneeled down. "Alexander, are you all right?" she asked, concerned.

"Alma, I can't believe it. You saved us!" Alexander said, looking into her eyes with admiration. "I never knew you

were so . . . so . . ."

Alma looked down at the ground and frowned. "So average?"

"So *above* average!" exclaimed Alexander. "So amazing! So awesome! And those are just the 'A' words!" He smiled broadly. He was in awe of Alma and how brave she had been.

73

Alma looked up and saw the sincerity in Alexander's eyes. She instantly felt better.

When the pair got to their feet, a book fell from Alexander's pocket to the ground. Alma's eyes widened as she picked it up.

"*The Secret Life of Horses?*" she said. "In paperback?"

"Yeah," said Alexander. "I've read it about a hundred times. That's where I found my horse's name. You know, Bucephalus was the horse of—"

"Alexander the Great!" Alma and Alexander said in unison.

Alexander couldn't believe Alma knew that historical fact.

"It's my favorite book in the whole world," Alma revealed.

Alexander gave her a knowing look. "I *knew* we had a lot in common."

Alma smiled warmly. Then she said, "Come on. Let's get you up this hill."

The pair headed to their horses and carefully made their way back up the ridge.

On their way back to Horseland, Alma and Alexander walked their horses on a wooded trail next to a calm brook.

Alma took a deep breath. "I'm sorry I wasn't honest with you, Alexander," she said. "I was so afraid you wouldn't like me."

A look of unease crossed Alexander's face. He realized it was time to tell the truth. "Well . . . you're not the only one," he admitted.

Alma was confused. "What do you mean?" she asked.

"Remember I wrote that I went to the state championship three times?" he asked.

"Yeah?" Alma said, her eyebrows raised with interest.

Alexander sighed. "The thing is, I just . . . went. With my parents. I sat in the stands. My folks work for a traveling carnival." He stuck his hands in his pockets, embarrassed. "We're not rich, not by a long shot."

Alma's face couldn't mask her surprise.

Alexander bowed his head and continued. "For some reason, everyone here seemed to think I was really special, and I never corrected them. What I know about horses, I read in my books."

Alma was surprised by the revelation, but she wasn't angry. "Alexander?" she said softly.

"Yeah, Alma?" replied Alexander, looking at her as he pushed his glasses back up on his nose.

Alma blushed and smiled warmly. "I think you're sorta . . . you know . . . you're not so average yourself."

Alexander's eyes grew wide and a big grin spread across his face. "You do?" he asked. Then he laughed and shook his head. "I mean, you don't?"

"Yeah," said Alma. "In fact, you're kinda . . . sorta . . . special."

Alexander beamed. *She kinda thinks I'm sorta special!* he thought excitedly. *If only I*

had been myself from the beginning!

Now Alexander hoped that the lies wouldn't prevent him and Alma from hanging out together. Biting his lip nervously, he asked, "I came here hoping you would teach me about horses. Do you think you still could?"

Alma walked to the edge of the brook and looked at her reflection for a moment. Beneath the silly clothes she was wearing, she could see the girl she always had been on the inside—strong, brave, and unique. It was time to get back to being herself—and liking it.

"Sure!" she told him. "I'll teach you everything I know about horses."

A hopeful look spread across Alexander's face. "So you're not *too* mad at me?"

Alma walked up to Alexander and put an arm around his shoulder. "How could I ever be mad at my pen pal?" she said. Then she looked him square in the eyes. "But let's promise to be honest with each other from

now on, okay?"

"Deal," agreed Alexander happily, and the two shook hands.

"Now, what do you say we head back to Horseland?" suggested Alma. She hopped up onto her horse's back. "Come on, Button! Yah!"

Alma and Button took off as Alexander scrambled to get onto Bucephalus.

"Hey, no fair! You got a head start!" Alexander called playfully.

"Well, hurry up, then!" Alma shouted back, as she rode through the woods.

CHAPTER 13

Shep, Teeny, and Angora sit on a grassy hill next to the Horseland ranch house.

"Now do you see why it's important to be yourself?" Shep asks Teeny. He hopes the story has made his point perfectly clear.

"You're right, Shep," Teeny says, nodding excitedly. "I am who I am, and who I am is . . . TEENY!" She marches around triumphantly. "I am pig, hear me *oooinnnk*!"

As Teeny jumps around and squeals,

Angora rolls her eyes. "Yeah, well, if you'll excuse me," she says with a sigh. "I have some more preening and grooming to do."

Shep looks at her with disappointment in his eyes. "Didn't you learn anything, Angora?" he asks.

"Yes," answers Angora. "I learned I have to be myself." She licks her paw. "And this is myself: preening and grooming."

Shep shakes his head. He can't believe it: Angora is right!

Meet the Riders and Their Horses

Sarah Whitney is a natural when it comes to horses. Sarah's horse, **Scarlet**, is a black Arabian mare.

Alma Rodriguez is confident and hard-working. Alma's horse, **Button**, is a skewbald pinto mare.

Molly Washington
has a great sense of
humor and doesn't
take anything
seriously—except her
riding. Molly's horse,
Calypso, is a spotted
Appaloosa mare.

Chloe Stilton
is often forceful and
very competitive, even
with her sister, Zoey.
Chloe's horse, **Chili**, is a
gray Dutch Warmblood
stallion.

Zoey Stilton
is Chloe's sister. She's
also very competitive
and spoiled. Zoey's
horse, **Pepper**, is a gray
Dutch Warmblood
mare.

Bailey Handler
likes to take chances.
His parents own
Horseland Ranch.
Bailey's horse, **Aztec**,
is a Kiger mustang
stallion.

Will Taggert is Bailey's cousin and has lived with the family since he was little. Because he's the oldest, Will is in charge when the adults aren't around. Will's horse, **Jimber**, is a palomino stallion.

Spotlight on Button

Breed: Skewbald Pinto

Physical Characteristics:
- Coat made up of white patches and another color
- White color on the legs, usually extending above the knees
- Four different body types: saddle, stock, hunter, and pleasure

Personality:
- Reliable
- Playful
- Disciplined
- Strong

Fun facts:
- If the color (other than white) is black, then the pinto is called a piebald.

- There are two pinto patterns: tobiano (a white horse with large spots of color) and overo (a colored horse with white jagged markings).
- Pintos' images have been found in Egyptian tombs that date as far back as the fourth century BC.

♡ Alma's ♡ Tips for Traveling with a Horse

Transporting your horse to shows or even just to the vet is an important job. Here are some helpful hints to consider before you hit the road.

Preparation

- Make sure your trailer is big enough for the horse to travel comfortably.

- Before a long trip, see the vet for a checkup and any vaccines that are due.
- Protect the horse with travel boots, a tail bandage, and a blanket appropriate for the weather.
- Have everything else packed and ready so that you can leave as soon as the horse is in the trailer.

Loading

- Make the trailer a place the horse will want to go into. Put some hay on the ramp and let in as much light as possible.
- Wear a riding helmet for protection.
- Lead the horse straight up the ramp.

On the Road

- Drive slowly and carefully.
- Avoid traveling during the hottest parts of the day.
- Offer the horse water and make sure the hay net is full.
- Make sure there's plenty of ventilation.

Unloading

- The vehicle and trailer should be parked.
- Make sure the ramp is stable.
- Lead the horse straight down the ramp.